MORE THAN 150,000 COPIES SOLD!

PRAISE FOR
THE JASMINE TOGUCHI SERIES

THREE JUNIOR LIBRARY GUILD SELECTIONS

FOUR CHICAGO PUBLIC LIBRARY'S BEST OF THE BEST BOOKS

AN AMAZON.COM BEST CHILDREN'S BOOK

TWO NERDY BOOK CLUB AWARDS

AN EVANSTON PUBLIC LIBRARY'S 101 GREAT BOOK FOR KIDS

A BANK STREET BEST CHILDREN'S BOOK OF THE YEAR

AN AMELIA BLOOMER LIST TITLE

A CBCC CHOICES LIST (BEST OF THE YEAR)

A BEVERLY CLEARY CHILDREN'S CHOICE AWARD NOMINEE

A 2021 NUTMEG BOOK AWARD NOMINEE

A ROMPER'S 100 PROGRESSIVE BOOK FOR CHILDREN

A CYBILS AWARD WINNER

A MARYLAND BLUE CRAB YOUNG READER AWARD WINNER FOR TRANSITIONAL FICTION

"In this new early chapter book series, Florence introduces readers to a bright character who is grappling with respecting authority while also forging her own path. Vuković's illustrations are expressive and imbue Jasmine and the Toguchi family with sweetness . . . This first entry nicely balances humor with the challenges of growing up; readers will devour it."

—*School Library Journal* on *Jasmine Toguchi, Mochi Queen*

"Adorable and heartwarming."

—*Booklist* on *Jasmine Toguchi, Mochi Queen*

ENJOY MORE ADVENTURES WiTH
JASMINE TOGUCHI

Jasmine Toguchi, Mochi Queen

Jasmine Toguchi, Super Sleuth

Jasmine Toguchi, Drummer Girl

Jasmine Toguchi, Flamingo Keeper

Jasmine Toguchi, Brave Explorer

JASMINE TOGUCHI

PEACE-MAKER

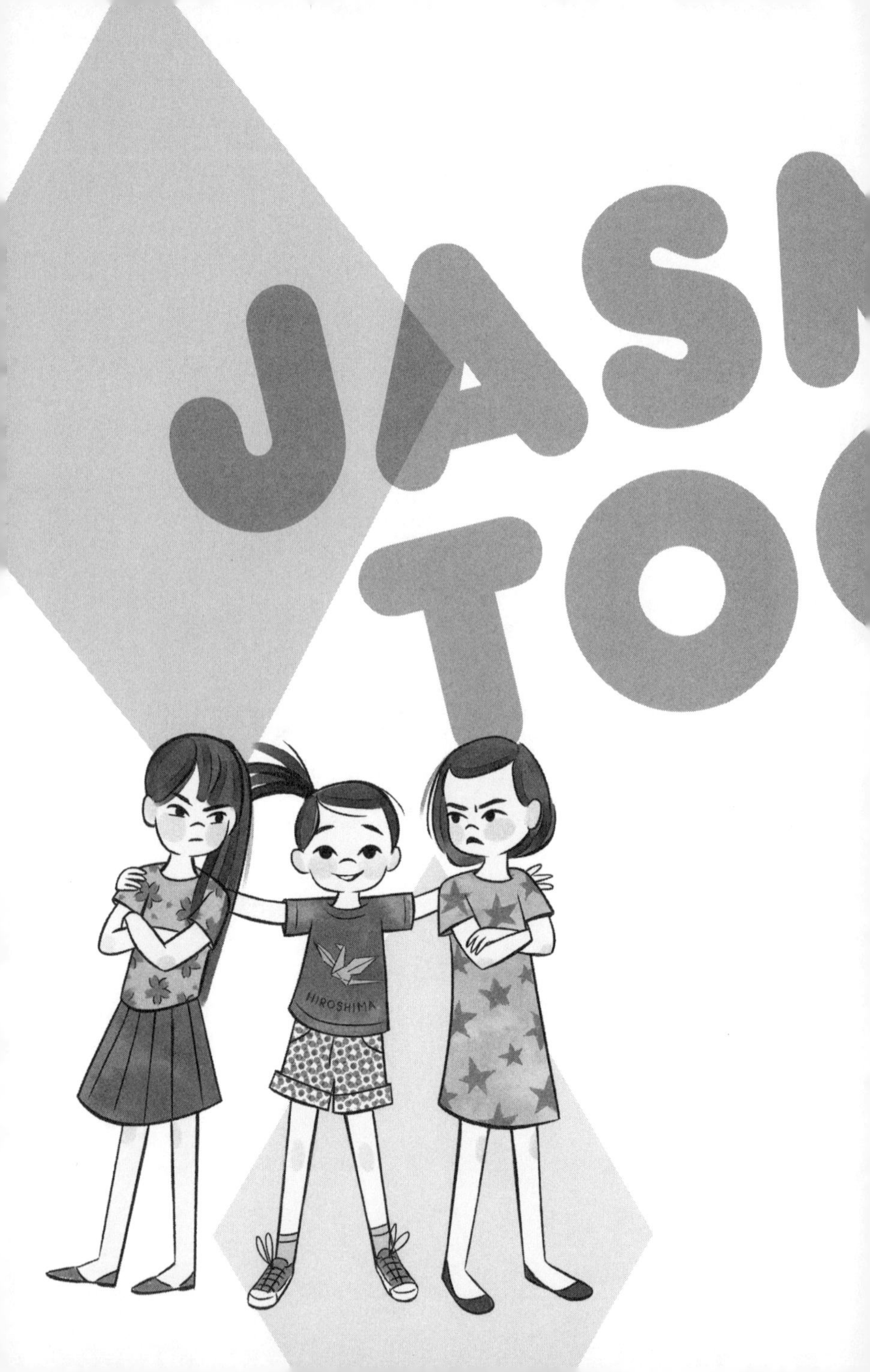
HIROSHIMA

MINE
GUCHI

PEACE-
MAKER

DEBBI MICHIKO FLORENCE PICTURES BY ELIZABET VUKOVIĆ

FARRAR STRAUS GIROUX • NEW YORK

Farrar Straus Giroux Books for Young Readers
An imprint of Macmillan Publishing Group, LLC
120 Broadway, New York, NY 10271 • mackids.com

Text copyright © 2023 by Debbi Michiko Florence
Illustrations copyright © 2023 by Elizabet Vuković
All rights reserved

Our books may be purchased for promotional, educational, or business use.
Please contact your local bookseller or the Macmillan Corporate and Premium
Sales Department at (800) 221-7945 ext. 5442 or by email at
MacmillanSpecialMarkets@macmillan.com.

Library of Congress Cataloging-in-Publication Data is available.

First edition, 2023
Book design by Angela Jun
Printed in the United States of America by Lakeside Book Company,
Crawfordsville, Indiana

ISBN 978-0-374-38934-5
10 9 8 7 6 5 4 3 2 1

IN LOVING MEMORY, FOR
MY OJIICHAN AND OBAACHAN
CHOTA AND TAKIKO
HIROKANE AND MY DAD,
DENTA HIROKANE —D.M.F.

FOR SADAKO SASAKI, FOR
CHILDREN IN WAR, FOR
HOPE —E.V.

CONTENTS

JASMINE TOGUCHI
PEACE-MAKER

TO OBAACHAN'S HOUSE WE GO!

The Tokyo train station was big. Very big! I followed Mom and Dad while dragging my suitcase behind me.

I, Jasmine Toguchi, was on the adventure of my life. I flew on a plane with my family all the way from our home in Los Angeles to Japan for a vacation. We spent two days in Tokyo doing fun things and eating yummy food. The best part so far was that my sister, Sophie, was mostly being nice to me. Normally Sophie, who is two years older than me, is bossy and doesn't like to hang out together. But now it seemed she liked spending time with me. It was as if Japan was magical and made wonderful things happen!

Today we were leaving Tokyo to go to Hiroshima to visit Obaachan. Usually we only see our grandma in January when she comes to our house for New Year's and stays for a whole month. This will be the first time we are visiting *her*! We walked and walked (there is a lot of walking to do in Japan) until at last we made it to our gate on the train platform.

"Did you know the Shinkansen is super-fast?" Sophie said in her teacher voice. It used to bother me. But now that Sophie was nicer to me, I liked learning from her. "Some people call it the bullet train."

"How fast does it go?" I asked.

"Fast," Sophie said.

Just as I was about to say that wasn't a good answer, our train pulled in. I couldn't wait to

board. I wanted to go super-fast! I followed
Mom and Dad and Sophie onto the train, and
we found our seats. Dad moved the backs of
the seats so that we could all face one another.
Sophie let me have the window seat. This
made me happy. Not only was I having a great
adventure like I wanted, but Sophie and I
were finally friends. Everything was perfect!

I hugged Fred Just Fred and stared out the
window. Fred Just Fred is my second-favorite
stuffed flamingo. My first favorite is Felicia,
but Mom wouldn't let me bring her because

she is just as tall as I am. I could see now that it would have been hard to carry her around. Like I said, we do a lot of walking in Japan.

The train pulled out of the station. We passed tall silver buildings and streets full of cars and more buildings. It seemed like we would never leave Tokyo. I waited and watched and waited and watched. After a long while there were fewer buildings and more open spaces.

"We're going fast!" I said as the train picked

up speed. "But it doesn't feel like it." The train was smooth and quiet.

"What are we going to do at Obaachan's?" I asked once the train was racing along outside of Tokyo. Fields and little houses flew by in a blur.

Mom looked up from her book and smiled. "We have some fun plans," she said. "But I think you will both enjoy spending time with Akari."

"Who is that?" Sophie asked.

"She is my cousin's daughter," Mom said. "She's a year older than Sophie and speaks English. Her father speaks both Japanese and English, so Akari has grown up speaking both languages."

"Awesome!" Sophie said.

"What is she like?" I asked. I hoped she enjoyed adventures, too.

"I haven't seen her since she was a baby," Mom said. "You'll have to tell me what she's like once you get to know each other."

This was super-great! I couldn't wait to get to Obaachan's, make a new friend, and have more adventures in Hiroshima!

"Are we there yet?" I asked Dad.

He smiled. "Maybe you and Sophie can play cards."

After three rounds of Uno, it was time to eat lunch. Mom had picked up bento boxes at the station before we got on the train. She got me a delicious tonkatsu sandwich. I had only had the fried pork cutlet with the yummy thick sauce on a plate at dinner. I wondered if I could put other dinner foods between bread to make lunch sandwiches. Like spaghetti!

Sophie and I played cards some more and then had reading time. Just when I thought we'd never get there, our train finally arrived in Hiroshima.

We took a taxi from the train station to Obaachan's house. As soon as the taxi stopped, Sophie and I piled out and gazed at the front of a little shop.

Wait a minute . . .

A JAPANESE HOME

"Obaachan lives in a shop!" I exclaimed. This was the coolest thing ever!

Obaachan stepped out of the store. She wore a gray dress with pretty blue flowers. Mom shouted, "Mama!" and ran to her.

My heart fluttered like a butterfly. I was so excited to see Obaachan! My feet acted before my brain. I ran to my grandma as soon as she was finished hugging Mom. I threw my arms around Obaachan and pressed my face against her. She smelled like trees. It was like taking a deep breath of fresh air. I felt safe and happy and warm.

"Misa-chan, welcome," Obaachan said, calling me by my Japanese middle name.

"My turn!" Sophie gently pushed me aside and hugged Obaachan.

"Hina-chan, yoku kitane."

Sophie had spent all summer studying Japanese. She and Obaachan had extra video calls where they spoke half the time in Japanese to help Sophie practice and the other half in English to help Obaachan practice. I thought about learning Japanese for the extra time with Obaachan, but then playing with my friends kept me too busy.

Dad bowed to Obaachan and she bowed to Dad.

"Come in," she said, and led the way into the shop.

There was a counter and a cash register by the front as we walked in. The store wasn't that big. There were three aisles full of cans and bottles. Along the back were doors that opened to refrigerated things. Would we eat by the shelves? Sleep in the aisles? Would Fred Just Fred keep watch by the cash register?

"Where do we sleep?" I asked, peering down an aisle.

"In the house, silly," Sophie said.

Normally Sophie would have said that in a mean voice. But when we were in Tokyo, I worked hard to be kind to Sophie. I even gave her a special present, and she ended up being nicer to me.

I wandered the three aisles of the little shop, look-ing at bottles of sauces, drinks, and canned foods. The words were in Japanese, but I used my super-sleuth skills. Most of the cans had pictures, so I recognized vegetables and fruits. Then something caught my attention.

"Sophie, look at this!" I shouted.

Sophie actually listened to me and hurried over to the big white freezer case.

"Ice cream?" she asked.

I slid open the top and we peered inside. "Ice cream!" I cheered.

But they didn't look like the ice cream bars we had at home.

"Ah-zoo-kee," Sophie said, sounding out the Japanese letters on a box. "Azuki! Jasmine, this ice cream is red bean."

"Would you girls like to try one?" Mom asked, walking over to us.

"Hai!" Sophie and I said yes at the same time.

"Dad and I will get the suitcases to our room," Mom said. "Do not leave the shop. If a customer comes in, call for Obaachan. She will be in the kitchen on the other side of the door."

Not only did we get to eat ice cream before dinner, but we got to watch the store all by ourselves. Best day ever!

Sophie and I unwrapped our bars.

"Wowee zowee! It's purple!" I waved the ice cream in the air.

Sophie laughed. "Yes, I know, it's your favorite color."

I bit into the cold ice cream bar. It was icy and sweet. And chewy. There were red beans in the ice cream. Delicious!

While we ate, I kept an eye on the shop. I hoped we would get a customer. But by the time we finished eating, not one shopper had stopped in.

Mom came to get us. "Obaachan wants to show you around the house."

You didn't have to ask me twice. I wiped my mouth with my hand and wiped my hand on my shorts. Sophie wrinkled her nose but didn't say anything. We walked over to the side of the shop where Dad was waiting on a raised platform.

"Take your shoes off here," he said. "And then you can come in."

Dad slid open a frosted glass door. We stepped into a kitchen.

"It's like Obaachan's house is part of the shop," I said. "That's so cool!"

The kitchen looked like any other kitchen. It was not very interesting.

Obaachan smiled at us. "I am so happy my granddaughters are here in my home," she said.

"Ureshii desu," Sophie said. She turned to me. "I said I am happy."

"Me too. I'm happy, too," I said.

"Your nihongo is getting very good," Obaachan said to Sophie.

Walnuts! I wish I had studied Japanese. I wanted Obaachan to say nice things to me, too.

"Come," she said in English at least. "Let me show you where you will sleep."

We followed her up the stairs and down a hallway. At the end of the hall, Obaachan slid open a door. The doors did not open in or out like at our house. Here, the doors reminded me of my best friend Linnie Green's sliding door that led to her backyard. But the doors in Obaachan's house were on the inside and looked like they were covered with paper. This door had paintings of maple leaves on it. So pretty! Maybe when I got home, I could paint a flamingo on my bedroom door.

"This is where your family will sleep," Obaachan said, leading us into the room.

It had tatami floors just like in the pictures Mom showed us before we left for Japan. They looked like straw mats. The only things in the room were our suitcases and a standing fan.

"Where are the beds?" I asked.

"Remember," Sophie said, using her teacher voice. "We are going to sleep on the floor."

"Oh yeah!" Mom told us about that. We will sleep on futons. In Japan, futons are not like the kind we have. In America, ours are more like a foldout couch than a sleeping mat.

Obaachan slid open another door, this time to a closet with shelves. She put a flannel sheet on the floor. Then she pulled out a colorful mattress. Obaachan unfolded the mattress and set it on the floor. We helped her put a sheet on it and tucked it under the mattress part.

"It is hot in the summer, so instead of a blanket or quilt, you will use this." Obaachan unfolded a towel the size of a blanket.

I loved the beds in Japan! The pillows felt like they had dried beans in them. Sophie and I helped Obaachan set up the rest of the futons. One for Dad, one for Mom, one for Sophie, and one for me. I made sure I got the light purple towel-blanket. We would all be sleeping in one room on the floor. Just like a slumber party! For the first time ever, I couldn't wait for bedtime.

Jasmine's Journal

Dear Linnie,

Guess what? Obaachan's house is super-cool. We get to eat on the floor! We sit on special pillows called zabuton. The table is really low. It's kind of like having a picnic in the house.

Even bath time is an adventure here. Remember how Ms. Sanchez taught us how to make lists in third grade? I am going to make a list now on how to take a bath in Obaachan's home.

1. Take off your clothes in a little room next to the bathtub room. Fold your clothes neatly (says Mom).

2. The tub is deep with a cover over it. Fold the cover back. The water in

the tub is super-hot, so it's all steamy when you open the cover.

3. Scoop out water with a plastic bowl. Obaachan's bowl is light blue with cute puppies on it. You can mix cold water into the hot water in your bowl. But do not put the cold water into the big tub (says Mom).

4. Splash yourself with the water. Mom said only till you are wet all over, but I liked splashing myself, so I did it a LOT. You can splash as much as you want because the floor is made of tile and has a big drain! If you want, you can sit on a low plastic stool. Sometimes I got tired of standing.

5. Scrub yourself with soap and a towel.

6. Scoop water out of the tub again and rinse off all the soap.

7. You can soak in the hot tub after. It was too hot for me (and kind of deep), so I did not do that part. But the grown-ups made a big deal about how good it felt.

8. Go out to the little room and dry off with a fluffy towel.

9. Put on your pj's if it's nighttime and your regular clothes if it's daytime. (Mom always makes me take a bath at night though.)

Linnie, it was so much fun! I wish our bath was like that at home. I think Mom saw what I was thinking and she told me not to try this when we got back to Los Angeles. Walnuts!

SQUIRT!

The next morning, I helped Mom put all the futons back into the closet while Dad and Sophie helped Obaachan make breakfast. In Japan, people put their futons away every morning and then take them out again at bedtime. That seemed like a lot of work. I told Obaachan she should leave the futons out all the time. She just laughed and patted my head. Maybe grown-ups liked to do extra work.

After we ate, Dad had a meeting with a professor at a college in Hiroshima. He had met with a teacher in Tokyo. Dad taught history at a college in Los Angeles. I guessed Dad liked to work on vacations.

I was going to get to work today, too. Obaachan said Sophie and I could help out at the store. I was so excited. I hopped twice on my left foot and three times on my right. I liked to hop and jump when I was excited. I would need the energy. This morning, Sophie and I were supposed to dust all the shelves in the store.

"Come on, Squirt," Sophie said. "Let's get to work."

Whoa. Sophie used to call me Squirt back when she was my age and I was in the first grade. She stopped calling me that over a year ago when we stopped hanging out together. She said I was too much of a baby to play with. Sophie only played with her friends, especially her best friend, Maya Fung. I didn't understand why she couldn't be friends with me at the same time. I had my best friend, Linnie, plus my other friends, but I still wanted to play with Sophie, too.

While Squirt might not sound like a nice name, I actually loved it. It was Sophie's special name for me.

"You take the low shelves and I'll take the high shelves," Sophie said, handing me a dustcloth.

Normally I did not like it when Sophie told me what to do. Normally Sophie would work as far away from me as possible. But like I said, we were friends now. She and I worked together in the same aisle. This made my heart fill with happiness.

When Linnie and I played together, we took turns coming up with things to do or how to do them. Sophie decided how we were dusting the shelves. I had an idea. But I was a little nervous to tell her. Normally only Sophie gets to make up what we do.

I took a big breath to calm my nerves. "Let's make this a game," I said.

Sophie looked at me while on her tiptoes dusting some cans. "What do you mean?"

Wowee zowee! She was listening to me! Before she could change her mind, I quickly said, "Let's have a race down the aisle to see who can dust the fastest."

"Okay, but we also have to do a good job. No cheating."

I put Fred Just Fred down on the counter next to the cash register. I needed to have both hands free to dust super-fast.

"Ready?" Sophie asked.

"Set," I said.

"Go!" we shouted at the same time, and then started dusting while scooting down the aisle.

"I won!" I yelled, jumping up and down.

"Just barely, Squirt." Sophie smiled. "Rematch?"

"Yes!"

We went down the next aisle. Sophie won that round. We started down the last aisle. We were halfway to the end, almost in a tie, when we heard someone call out, "Ohayo!"

AKARI

Sophie and I froze.

A woman wearing a gray skirt and white blouse peeked her head into the aisle. Was she a customer?

She smiled. "Sayuri Obachan desu. Hajime mashite!" She bowed. "Hina-chan. Misa-chan."

Sophie bowed and said, "Ohayo gozai masu."

I copied her and said good morning in

Japanese, too. This was Mom's cousin Sayuri! I wondered where Akari was. I couldn't wait to meet her.

I knew that Sophie and I would have great fun with our cousin!

"Akari-chan!" Sayuri Obachan called.

Akari pranced into the aisle and stood next to her mom. Wait! She was holding Fred Just Fred!

Akari turned to her mom. "Korega hoshii."

Sophie glanced at me and whispered, "I think she thinks it's for sale. She just told her mom she wants it."

NO! I ran up to Akari and tried to snatch my flamingo back, but she wouldn't let go. She scowled at me and held Fred Just Fred out of my reach.

"Hey," I said, pointing at Fred Just Fred. "He is mine!" I did remember that pointing was rude in Japan, but right now I was too upset to care.

Sophie stepped up next to me. "Misa-chan no mono desu," Sophie said. She firmly took Fred Just Fred away from Akari and handed him back to me. My sister! My hero! I hugged Fred Just Fred.

"Gomen nasai." Akari said she was sorry.

It was a misunderstanding. She didn't know Fred Just Fred belonged to me. I had left him next to the cash register after all.

"It's okay," I said.

"Sayuri-san!" Mom stepped into the store. Mom and Sayuri Obachan laughed with happiness, the way Linnie and I did when we saw each other after a weekend apart. They started speaking in Japanese very quickly. I glanced at Sophie, who shrugged.

"Hi. I am Akari." Akari smiled at Sophie.

"I'm Hina," she said and then nodded to me. "My sister, Misa."

"Nice to meet you," Akari said, still only looking at Sophie.

"Girls," Mom called us over. "Would you like to work in the store or go into the house and play? Obaachan is getting a snack together."

"Come," Akari said, linking her arm through Sophie's and tugging her toward the house. "We eat."

Sophie glanced back at me. "Come on, Squirt."

I squeezed Fred Just Fred. My insides felt weird and squishy. "I want to work in the shop," I said.

I watched Sophie go with Akari. They took off

their shoes and climbed onto the platform. They were talking and laughing as they went into the house.

Jasmine's Journal

Dear Linnie,

Guess what? I got to work in a store! Sayuri Obachan is super-nice. *Obachan* is a way to say "aunt." You can use it for all women relatives and friends.

I rang up customers on the cash register. A lady bought salad dressing, milk, and yogurt drinks in little bottles. I want to try some later. A businessman in a suit bought iced coffee in a can. And a mom with a baby strapped to her back bought toilet paper and diapers. I also put price stickers on cans! It was super-fun!

Tomorrow we are going to go to an island called Miyajima. We will take a ferry! So far I've been on

a plane, a train, a subway, the Shinkansen (a super-fast train), a taxi, and now a ferry! I can't wait!

P.S. I think Sophie and I are good friends now. Don't worry. You will always be my best friend!

P.P.S. I met Sayuri Obachan's daughter, Akari.

FERRY ADVENTURE

I hardly slept because I was excited for our next adventure. Mostly I was excited to spend time with Sophie and our cousin Akari. I had not been able to play with Akari yet since I worked in the store yesterday, while Sophie and Akari hung out in the house. Today I would become friends with Akari, too!

The ferry boat had three levels. The bottom one was for cars. The next level had an indoor cabin. The very top was outdoors.

I led the way up three flights of stairs. I was surprised when everyone followed me, even Sophie. Sophie did not like to be up high. It made her nervous. But the ferry wasn't as high as Tokyo Tower, at least.

Everyone sat down on the benches. I wanted to stand at the rail and watch the water below.

"Come on, Sophie," I said as the ferry pulled away from the dock.

Sophie and Akari were glued together, it seemed. The only time Sophie talked to me yesterday was after Akari and Sayuri Obachan left.

"Sophie!" I called again. It was like I was invisible.

They were looking at something on Akari's phone. I walked over and sat next to Sophie. When I tried to look at Akari's phone, she put it away in her purse. They leaned close together and talked quietly to each other.

I walked over to the adults. "Does someone want to stand at the railing with me?" I asked.

Dad smiled. "That sounds like a good idea, Jasmine."

Standing with Dad was even better than standing with Sophie would have been. The ferry was slow, but it was fun looking down. The water churned and splashed against the sides of the ferry. We left the city of Hiroshima behind. Before I could get bored, Dad nudged me.

"Look over there, Jasmine," Dad said. "That's the torii, or gate, for Itsukushima Shrine. It's one of the most famous sites in Japan."

"Is the torii floating on the water?" I asked, staring at the pretty red gate.

"It looks like that, doesn't it?" Dad said. "At high tide, the water goes up and past the torii to the shoreline. We won't be able to walk

around it like during low tide. But I think it's prettiest like this."

"I think so, too," I agreed.

We floated past the gate, and as soon as the ferry docked, I tugged Dad off the boat. We followed the crowd away from the pier into the town.

"Wowee zowee," I said. "Are those deer?"

I counted—ichi, ni, san—three cute little

deer. The deer walked with the crowd like they were sightseeing, too.

"This island is known for the tame sika deer," Dad said. "They're used to people, but don't get too close. They are still wild animals."

We caught up to the

rest of our family. Sophie and Akari walked together.

"What are we doing today?" I asked Obaachan.

"We are visiting a famous shrine, a famous temple, and eating delicious food," she said, taking my hand.

I used to think shrines and temples sounded boring. But after we visited one in Tokyo, I learned they are interesting.

As we walked around, I tried not to care that Akari used her phone to take selfies of only her and Sophie. Dad took plenty of pictures of me. I tried not to care that when we got special treats called momiji manju, Sophie and Akari shared. The manju was shaped like maple leaves. It was cake on the outside with delicious fillings. Sophie got chocolate. Akari got anpan. They broke theirs in half and traded to share.

I ordered anpan, too. Azuki bean paste is my favorite mochi filling.

"Can I taste some of your chocolate?" I asked Sophie.

"Oh, I ate mine already," she said. "Hey, Akari-chan, can you give Misa-chan a taste of your half?"

Akari shoved the rest of the cake into her mouth. She chewed and made an *Oops, sorry* face. She smiled. Then she hooked her arm through Sophie's and took her away, leaving me standing alone with my maple leaf manju.

"Misa-chan?" Obaachan held up half of her treat. "Do you want to share with me? I got matcha."

I blinked and turned away from Sophie and Akari, who were skipping together down the

walkway. Obaachan looked at me with warm, kind eyes. I traded halves with Obaachan even though I didn't love green tea filling. I did not want to hurt her feelings. I wanted to be kind even if Akari was not.

"Akari-chan is not used to sharing," Obaachan said as we sat on a bench to eat.

"It's fine," I said even though it wasn't. I would not let Akari ruin my adventure.

SECOND CHANCES

We went to a small restaurant for lunch. I wanted to sit next to Sophie. When I tried to sit in the chair beside her, Akari scooted right into it.

"Misa-chan," Obaachan called to me. "Sit here."

I smiled. Sitting with Obaachan would be even better. But before I was able to get to her, Akari popped out of her chair and ran over to sit by Obaachan. I huffed. I couldn't believe that just two days ago I was excited to meet Akari. She was very hard to be around.

I quickly sat down beside Sophie. But Sophie looked upset.

"Can I change places with you, Mom?" she asked.

My heart fell into my stomach as Mom and Sophie switched chairs. Now Sophie was sitting next to Akari and Akari was sitting next to Obaachan. I loved Mom and Dad for sure, but I really wanted to sit with Obaachan. I didn't get to see her very often. Just once a year when she came to our house for a month at New Year's. This was the first time we were in Japan. Akari got to see Obaachan all the time!

Also, even though Sophie and I saw each other all the time at home, this was the first time in forever she was being nice to me. Akari was not only stealing Obaachan away from me but Sophie, too!

I needed to take Akari out of my adventure.

Or at least make Sophie see that Akari wasn't as nice as me. I needed to help her remember our fun times.

"Hey, Sophie," I said during lunch. "Remember when we had an edamame war?"

Sophie barely looked at me.

"Do you want my dessert, Sophie?" I asked, holding up a little cookie that came with my tea.

Again, Sophie didn't seem to hear me. She was too busy talking with Akari.

After lunch, we walked to the Daisho-in Temple. Along the stone steps leading to the temple were a lot of stone statues that were shorter than me.

"Look at these cute statues," I said. "Why are they all wearing hats?"

"There are five hundred of these Buddhist statues," Obaachan said.

Mom nodded. "I believe the local residents knit hats for them every year as an offering."

"That's awesome," I said. I turned to Sophie. "Isn't that interesting?"

Just as it seemed like Sophie was going to talk with me, Akari grabbed her hand and pulled her ahead of us. I was tired of Akari. I did not want to be kind. I did not want to be polite. I wanted to tell Akari to get her own sister and leave mine alone! But I knew Mom and Dad would not be happy with me if I did that.

Three more days until we left for our next adventure. I could put up with Akari until then. Obaachan was coming with us, but

Akari would stay behind with her mom. Good thing.

At least I had Obaachan to myself for now. I took a deep breath to calm down, like Dad taught me. I counted to ten. I would not let Akari ruin my adventure.

"What are we doing next?" I asked Obaachan.

Obaachan smiled. "I think you will like this." She raised her eyes to the sky.

I looked up to see little cars on cables moving high up the mountain.

"Wowee zowee! Do we get to ride those?" I hopped on my left foot five times and jumped up and down twice. I was so excited! Too bad I left Fred Just Fred at the house. I was afraid Akari would take him again. He would have loved to have been high in the sky.

"The cable cars take us to the top for spectacular views," Mom said. "I know how much you like that."

"It will be like flying!" I shouted.

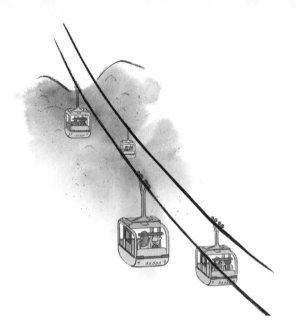

"Is there another way to go up?" Sophie asked in a quiet voice.

Oh yes. Sophie was afraid of being up high. I was a good super sleuth. I could tell by the way Sophie frowned and clenched her fists that she was not happy.

"It is the best way," Akari said.

I read a sign that was in Japanese and English. I smiled. "Look, Sophie! There is a hiking trail that goes up. We can walk!"

"No." Akari crossed her arms. "It takes too long to walk."

"Then we don't have to go," I said.

"Misa-chan, kowai?" Akari asked with a mean smile.

I knew that word. She thought I was afraid. I was not afraid! But before I could answer, Sophie made a small sound. I heard Dad's voice in my head to be kind. I would not rat out my sister. But I also really wanted to go up and see the views.

"We don't have enough time to hike up," Mom said. Mom was smart. She knew I was not afraid. She knew I did not want to make Sophie feel bad.

Sayuri Obachan said something in Japanese. Mom translated into English for me. "Sayuri Obachan said she will wait here with you. She has been up many times."

I started to shake my head. I wanted to go up! But then Sophie came over to me and took my hand. "I will stay with Jasmine."

That made me happy!

"Hina-chan," Akari said. "Leave your baby

sister here. We will have fun going to the top together."

Sophie shook her head. "I will stay with my sister."

Akari glared at me and then stomped off, holding Obaachan's hand. I was a little sad I

would not get to ride the car in the sky. But I was happy that Sophie wanted me to stay with her. I was happy to spend time alone with my sister.

"Akari is not very nice," I said softly so Sayuri Obachan would not hear me.

"She's not so bad, Jasmine," Sophie said. "Just give her a chance."

I would have given her a chance. The problem was Akari was not giving *me* a chance.

Jasmine's Journal

A good friend:

1. Is kind

2. Doesn't leave others out

3. Shares her food and toys

4. Likes to do the same things

5. Is fun to be around

6. Is not Akari

BOSSY PANTS

The day after we went to Miyajima was a resting day, even though I didn't need to rest. Sayuri Obachan had to work in the store since they closed it for our day of fun. I hoped Akari would stay at her house, but nope. She showed up with her mom bright and early after breakfast.

Akari came bursting into the house like she lived there.

"Look!" She sat down on the floor next to

Sophie, who was reading a new manga. It was in Japanese, so it took her a very long time.

Sophie put down her book as Akari took out a DVD from her backpack. I wanted to see, too. I leaned over. Akari tucked it against her chest to hide it from me.

I remembered Sophie asked me to give Akari a chance. Even though Akari didn't know how to be a good friend, I did.

"I like your backpack," I said.

Akari didn't say anything. She walked over to the small television. She slid the disc into the player and switched on the TV.

Then she turned to me with her hands on her hips. "Misa-chan, this movie is not for you. You should leave."

"I am not leaving," I said, crossing my arms. I scooted closer to Sophie.

"Fine. You will be sorry," Akari said. She picked up the remote and then squished between me and Sophie to sit down. I had to move over or she would have sat down right on top of me. *Walnuts!*

She turned to Sophie. "This is one of my favorite movies. You will love it."

Akari wiggled around and moved her arms so that her elbow jabbed me. I moved even farther away from her. But not too far, so I could still see the TV.

Spooky music played over a dark screen.

The music got louder and louder. And then someone screamed and made all of us jump. Akari giggled. Then a cartoon face flashed on the screen. It was a lady with scraggly hair and scary eyes. I liked scary movies as much as the next kid, but I knew one kid who did not.

Sophie had her hands over her eyes. Akari looked at Sophie and put the movie on pause. Fortunately it was on a scene of a forest without that scary lady.

"Hey, Hina-chan," Akari said, tugging on Sophie's hands. "You can't see if you cover your eyes."

 I have known Sophie all my life. I know she hates being scared. She won't even watch funny cartoons about cute ghosts at home. This one for sure did not look funny or cute.

I spoke up. "Our mom has a rule that we are not allowed to watch scary shows." This was not a real rule. But it felt like it could be a Mom rule.

"This is not your mom's house," Akari said. "I am allowed to watch whatever I want."

"Come on, Sophie," I said. I stood up. Sophie did, too, and gave me a small smile. But before she could follow me out of the room, Akari grabbed her arm.

"No. Stay here, Hina-chan. You watch the movie with me."

"I need to go with Misa-chan," Sophie said. She tried to move, but Akari would not let go of her.

"I am older than you. You have to do what I say," Akari said to Sophie.

Whoa. That was what Sophie said to me a lot at home. I glanced at Sophie. Her face got dark like storm clouds gathering in the sky.

"You are not the boss of me! I don't have to

listen to you!" Sophie used the voice I had heard many times back at home, except this time she wasn't shouting at me.

Akari let go of Sophie. She stood up, too. They were face-to-face.

"You are in my house," Akari said. "You have to do what I say!"

"This isn't your house. It's my obaachan's house," Sophie said. She turned so quickly, her skirt fluffed up. She stalked over to where I was standing. My mouth was open in surprise. I bet I looked like my pet fish back at home.

Sophie took my hand and pulled me out of the room. "Come on, Jasmine. Let's do something together."

I flashed a smile at Akari and followed my sister out.

JUST THE TWO OF US

For the rest of the day, Sophie and I stayed in the room where we slept. She set up the futons on their sides, like walls, and made two houses. One for me and one for her. We put the towel-blankets on the floor and made them rugs for our houses. I used my pillow to make a bed for Fred Just Fred.

"I'll be right back," Sophie said.

I wondered if she decided to make up with Akari. Maybe she would invite her to play with us. I tried not to feel disappointed. I knew if Akari joined us, she would push me out. Sophie was finally playing with me. I was having fun again.

"Look what I have, Squirt." Sophie came back into the room. She was carrying a tray. Balanced on it were two teacups and a little bowl of senbei. I loved rice crackers! She took the tray into her pretend house.

"Come over and visit me," she called out. "We can have teatime."

I grabbed Fred Just Fred and pretended to knock on Sophie's door.

"Come in!" she called.

Sophie set the tray on the floor. I sat across from her. She glanced at my stuffed flamingo.

"I'm sorry, Fred Just Fred," Sophie said. "I didn't bring a drink for you. But here is a

snack." She picked out a shrimp chip from the bowl and put it in front of Fred Just Fred.

Sophie and I smiled at each other. I was happy that she and Akari were in a fight. Just two more days until we left Akari behind!

After we finished our snacks, Sophie came to my pretend house for reading time. Fred Just Fred took a nap.

"Girls!" Mom's voice floated up the stairs. "Lunchtime!"

"We should clean up," Sophie said. "Together."

Doing anything with Sophie made me happy, even though I was not a fan of cleaning up. It felt like we were a team.

When we got downstairs, Akari was sitting by herself at the table.

"Sophie and Jasmine," Mom said, "could you come in here and help me?"

We walked into the kitchen. Mom had that wrinkle on her forehead that meant she was annoyed. It was the first time in a long time she looked annoyed with both of us at the same time.

"Where were you two?" Mom asked. "I found Akari watching TV all by herself."

Sophie was quiet. She nibbled her lip. I knew that meant she was nervous.

"Akari was watching a scary movie," I said. "So we went upstairs."

Mom shook her head. "You should have

invited Akari to join you. She said you both left her there. Alone."

"We're sorry, Mom," I said.

"I expect you to play nicely together. It's not kind to leave someone out," Mom said.

It was my turn to nibble my lip. Not because I was nervous, but because I wanted to keep the words from flying out of my mouth. I knew if I told Mom that Akari was the one leaving *me* out, it would sound like I was making excuses. Plus, I could tell from Mom's face that she was not in a listening mood.

"Yes, Mom," Sophie finally said.

I did not make any promises. The longer Sophie was mad at Akari, the more time I would have with Sophie alone. And to be honest, I did not think the three of us could play together nicely.

PLAYTiME. NOT.

After lunch, Obaachan took me, Sophie, and Akari to a nearby park. Well, Obaachan *said* it was nearby, but to me it felt like we walked a billion miles in the baking sun.

Akari walked in front of us, leading the way. She was stomping her feet on the sidewalk with her hands in fists. Sophie followed right behind Akari, trying to keep up. I didn't understand why Sophie wanted to walk so close to Akari. I walked next to Obaachan, happy to have her to myself.

"When we get back, can we have some ice cream?" I asked Obaachan. Thinking about a nice cold treat made me feel a little less hot.

"Hai," she said.

We finally got to the park. Obaachan sat on a bench in the shade. Akari sat by herself on the swings.

"Hey, Sophie," I said. "They have a seesaw!"

I'd seen them in pictures before, but I had never been on one. Our park at home didn't have a seesaw. It looked like fun. Sophie shook her head. Right. She did not like to go up high. She did not even like to swing on swings. But to my surprise, she sat down on the swing right next to Akari.

I climbed a tower to the second highest platform. I sat on a bench in front of a puzzle. I pretended to do the puzzle by spinning the shapes, but I was really watching Sophie and Akari. I did not understand why Sophie chose to sit on the swing. She did not like to swing. Why did she sit next to Akari? Sophie was mad at Akari. And Akari was mad at Sophie.

After a few minutes, Akari got up and walked over to the seesaw. I really wanted to do the seesaw. But not with her. Sophie stayed on the swing. She looked sad. She was watching Akari. It made me think Sophie was not really mad at Akari. It made me think Sophie wanted to be friends with Akari again.

But I did not want that at all!

I climbed higher to the very top of the tower. Sophie stayed on the swing, rocking back and forth, but her toes never left the ground. I circled the tower. I had left Fred Just Fred at home, but now I wished

I had brought him. He would love it here, high up in the sky.

I heard a noise behind me and quickly swung around. It was Akari. What was she doing up here? I did not want to share the tower with her.

"You are not afraid," Akari said suddenly.

"What do you mean?" I held on to the rail, ready to climb down to the ground. To Obaachan. To Sophie.

"You are not afraid." She said it again. This time she waved her hand over the side of the tower.

"No, I am not afraid of being high up," I said.

"You are not afraid of scary movies," she said.

I nibbled my lip. If I told her that I was not

afraid of scary movies, then Akari might figure out it was Sophie who was afraid. I did not want to make Sophie look bad.

"Do you want to do the seesaw with me?" Akari pointed down at the playground.

My feet tickled. They wanted to hop and jump. I really wanted to ride a seesaw. And maybe Akari would be my friend now.

I peeked over the railing at the playground. Sophie was watching us. Akari saw this, too. She put her arm around me so that Sophie could see.

"Come on, Misa-chan," she said very loudly. "Let's play together."

Sophie quickly looked at her feet but not before I saw her face. She was sad. I did not want to make Sophie sad. Akari did not seem to care that she was hurting Sophie's feelings. She did not care that she had hurt *my* feelings. Maybe Akari liked to be in a fight. I did not.

I climbed down without answering Akari.

Mom would say I was not being kind, but Akari wasn't very kind either.

When we finally walked back home, Obaachan told us we could pick ice cream for ourselves out of the freezer. She told us to eat together in the kitchen. She wanted to throw us together, but we would not stick.

It was very tiring being in the same room and not talking. The store closed at seven p.m. every night. Then Sayuri Obachan and Akari would go home to have dinner with Akari's dad. We would finally be free of Akari and eat our dinner. But I was so tired that I was ready for bed. That is saying a lot because I never feel like I am ready for bed.

Jasmine's Journal

Dear Linnie,

Tomorrow we are going to a special park called Peace Park. It will be a new adventure! Maybe this park will have roller coasters and waterslides!

The best thing is that Akari is not coming with us. She said she's already been to Peace Park many times and didn't want to go. Her mom, Sayuri Obachan, has to watch the store anyway.

The name Peace Park sounds perfect. It will feel peaceful (and fun) not to have Akari there.

PEACE PARK

We took a bus to Peace Park. I added "bus" to my list of things I have traveled on in Japan. More adventure for me! When we got there, I was full of happy energy. I skipped and hopped while holding Dad's hand.

"Goodness, Jasmine," Mom said. "You sure are in a great mood."

"I am in a super-duper happy hoppy magnificent mood!" I shouted. We were finally free of Akari. I had my family to myself. I had Sophie to myself.

Sophie did not look as happy as I felt. She walked alone, dragging her feet. Her shoulders were slumped. Maybe she was just hot and tired. It seemed like it was always hot in Japan.

I let go of Dad's hand and caught up to Sophie.

"What's wrong?" I asked.

She shrugged.

"Are you hot? Tired? Mad? Sad?" I tried to be a super sleuth.

"Jasmine," Sophie said in the voice she used to use back at home. "Just leave me alone."

Fine. I left her alone and walked with Obaachan.

When we arrived at the park, there were a lot of people there. All around me I heard different languages. I recognized English and Japanese. I heard some Spanish. Our third-grade teacher, Ms. Sanchez, taught us some Spanish words. There were people from all over the world here.

"Why is this park so special?" I asked. I did

not see any swings or seesaws, roller coasters or waterslides.

Dad led us to a crowd in front of a big stone arch. Everyone was quiet, using their library voices to talk, even though we were outdoors. When it was our turn to stand in front of the arch, Dad held my hand, and with his other, he held Sophie's.

"See that building through the arch?" he asked.

The stone arch was like a frame for the building in the distance. The building had a dome with no roof. It looked like a skeleton. It had no windows or doors, just openings that looked like empty eyes.

"What's wrong with it?" I asked. "Are they still building it?"

"Why does it look so beat-up?" Sophie asked.

Usually when Sophie and I asked a lot of questions, Dad loved to answer us. He is a

teacher of history. He loves to tell us about things that happened in the past. But for the first time, he didn't answer quickly.

Dad took a big breath and squeezed my hand. "Some time ago, before you were born and even before I was born, there was a big war called World War II. At that time, Japan and the United States were fighting each other."

I gasped.

Dad continued, "The United States dropped the first ever atomic bomb, or A-bomb, right here on Hiroshima." Dad squeezed my hand again. Mom put her hands on Sophie's shoulders. "Many, many people died."

"Dad! That's terrible!" Sophie gasped.

"I know," he said sadly. "That building was one of the few that remained standing. It now serves as a memorial to remind all of us of the horrifying destruction caused by the A-bomb."

I stared at the building. I thought about how scary it must have been to have a bomb drop on the city.

"Why?" I asked. I wasn't even sure what I was asking. Why were Japan and the United States fighting? Why did the United States drop a horrible bomb on Japan? Why did they want to kill people? So many *whys* clogged my throat. It made my eyes watery.

"There is no easy answer to that really good question, Jasmine," Dad said. "The United States and Japan both hurt each other during the war. After the war, the United States helped Japan rebuild. The two countries slowly learned to trust each other. But it took a lot of work and time."

Mom wrapped her arms around Sophie and me and hugged us. "This whole area is called the Peace Memorial Park. It is a reminder of the importance of peace and that no good comes from fighting."

We stared quietly at the broken building. My heart felt sad.

"Come," Mom said.

We walked with our family to another part of the park. We stopped at a tall, skinny stone dome. At the very top was a metal statue of a little girl. Her arms were raised and she was carrying a giant metal origami crane.

"This is a memorial for all the children who lost their

lives because of the A-bomb," Dad said. "Another important reminder for peace."

For the first time ever, I did not have words. I didn't feel like hopping and skipping anymore. My arms and legs felt heavy like stone.

We walked around the park to a pretty river. A man was playing a piano right by the water. I thought to ask how the piano got there. But instead, I let the music wash over me as I stood with my family.

It was beautiful. It was peaceful.

PEACE-MAKER

When we got back to Obaachan's house, everyone stopped in the store to talk to Sayuri Obachan. Sophie dug around in the freezer for an ice cream bar. My stomach was still full of sadness. I did not want to eat ice cream. I took off my shoes and went into the house.

Akari was sitting at the kitchen table, hunched over a notebook. Her pencil moved in smooth strokes. This made me curious.

"What are you doing?" I asked, sitting next to her.

Akari slammed her notebook closed. That's when I remembered that I did not like Akari. She was not very nice.

When I stood up to leave, Akari opened her notebook again. I peeked at the page.

"Is that a picture of a house?" I asked.

Akari slowly turned the notebook so that I could see better. It was a drawing of Obaachan's house and store.

"Wowee zowee, that is really good." That was the truth.

"Thank you," she said softly.

"I'm pretty good at drawing, too," I said.

Akari tore a sheet of paper from her notebook and slid it across the table. I sat down again and grabbed a pencil. I drew Fred Just Fred.

We were quiet as we drew. The sound of our pencils on paper reminded me of water sounds. And that reminded me of the river in Peace Park and the pretty piano music. It felt . . . peaceful.

Peace. Dad said during the war, Japan and the United States were fighting. Mom said fighting was hurtful. Dad also said that it took work and time to become friends. I glanced at Akari. I was still angry that Akari was mean to me. But I also knew Sophie was feeling hurt, too. Could it be that Akari was feeling hurt?

"Sophie seems sad," I said.

Akari drew a pretty Japanese garden with rocks and pebbles and a small tree. When she was almost finished, she said, "I wish I had a sister or a brother or even a pet."

I thought about how sometimes Sophie wasn't very nice to me or bossed me around or showed off how much she knew. But also she was almost always around and I could talk to her. Even if she didn't talk back. Sometimes she surprised me with gifts. She looked out for me. I was glad she was my sister. Now it was my turn to look out for her. I wanted her to be happy.

"I will be right back," I said to Akari.

I went into the store. Sophie was sitting on a stool behind the cash register, finishing her ice cream bar.

"Did you get to ring up any customers?" I asked, leaning on the counter.

"I did! A lady bought an ice cream bar like mine for her little boy. He

was so cute! And I spoke Japanese with her." Sophie smiled.

I liked seeing my sister smile. "I was talking to Akari in the house."

Sophie's smile disappeared.

I kept going. "Did you know she is an artist?"

"I don't care," Sophie said.

"Akari seems sad about your fight," I said. "I think she is lonely because she is not as lucky as I am to have a sister."

Sophie raised her eyebrows at me.

"We leave tomorrow. It will probably be a very long time before you see each other again," I said.

Sophie shrugged.

"Fighting is bad, like Mom said," I told her. "Maybe it would be better if we both made up with Akari."

"When did you get so smart, Squirt?" Sophie asked.

I grinned.

Sophie and I went into the house and sat down with Akari. She did not look up from her drawing.

"Hey, Akari," I said. "I told Sophie how you are good at drawing."

Akari finished her picture and then tore the sheet of paper from her notebook. She slid it over to us. It was a picture of three girls standing inside Obaachan's shop. I knew which one I was because the smallest girl held a stuffed flamingo that looked like Fred Just Fred. The other two girls had their arms over each other's shoulders and were smiling.

"This is very good," I said. I nudged Sophie.

She cleared her throat. "I don't like scary movies," Sophie said in a small voice. "I am afraid of ghosts and high-up places. I also don't like the dark or small spaces." Sophie looked at me. "Misa-chan is more like you. She's brave."

"Sometimes I get nervous when I don't know things," I said. "Like not knowing we are not supposed to talk on the subway in Japan."

"I don't know how to swim," Akari said quietly. "I am afraid of water."

"I guess there are things we are all afraid of," I said.

"And we are all brave in our own ways," Sophie said.

"Maybe we can stop fighting," I said.

Akari nodded and we all smiled at one another.

"Can we draw something together?" I asked.

Akari tore out two pages from her notebook and handed one each to me and Sophie. She took out pretty colored pencils from her bag and put them on the table between us.

Akari, Sophie, and I drew together while we talked about all the things we liked to do. We did not fight for the rest of the day. We were nice to one another.

Peace felt good.

Jasmine's Journal

Dear Linnie,

Writing letters to you in my journal inspired me to tell Akari and Sophie that they should write letters to each other. Akari will write in English and Sophie will write in Japanese so they can practice. I am happy for them!

It turns out Akari is not so bad after all. Now all three of us are friends. (But you are a much, much better friend!)

Tomorrow we are going to Kabo. It is a small fishing village. Mom says this is where Obaachan grew up. Obaachan is very old, so her house must be very old, too. I wonder if it has electricity. We might have to use candles like in the old days!

Maybe Obaachan will show us her old toys?
Maybe she had a special thinking tree? I hope
she lets me climb it! I'm so excited for my next
adventure!

AUTHOR'S NOTE

On August 6, 1945, the United States, in an attempt to end World War II and force Japan's surrender, dropped the first ever atomic bomb onto the city of Hiroshima. The effects were devastating. The bomb killed hundreds of thousands of people at the time of impact— and afterward, from injuries and radiation poisoning. Today the Hiroshima Peace Memorial Park and Museum sits at ground zero. The arch that Jasmine and her family visit in the Peace Park is a monument with a stone chest that holds the names of more than 290,000 victims.

I was a little older than Jasmine when I first visited the museum and park. It made me very sad.

However, I have many happy childhood memories of visiting my paternal grandparents and relatives in Hiroshima. My aunt and uncle lived in a house very similar to the one Jasmine visits in this book. They also had a store attached to their home, and I loved being able to help ring up customers. My sister and I ate many ice cream bars there.

One of my favorite memories of my grandpa is at Miyajima. I was probably close to Jasmine's age and in such a happy mood to visit Miyajima that I wanted to spin. So I took his hand and spun my ojiichan around and around in a circle, and he spun along with me. My parents caught this on a movie camera. At first Ojiichan didn't seem to want to spin, but it showed me how much he loved me. I am grateful to have had time with my grandparents in Japan. I wanted Jasmine to make happy memories with her obaachan in Japan, too.

HOW TO MAKE AN ORIGAMI DOVE

Sadako Sasaki was two years old when the A-bomb dropped onto her home city of Hiroshima. She survived the initial bombing but became very sick from radiation poisoning. When she was twelve years old and in the hospital, she folded a thousand paper cranes in the hopes that it would bring her luck and heal her. And although she did not get better, people remember her to this day and fold cranes in her honor. Today an origami crane symbolizes peace.

Folding the origami crane can be challenging for small hands, but with an adult's help, perhaps you, too, can make an origami crane like Sadako did so very long ago. You can learn more about Sadako online as well as find instructions for how to make an origami crane.

An origami dove is easier to make. Doves can also symbolize love and peace. Here are instructions for folding an origami dove.

MATERIALS

- Square paper
- Scissors
- Pens and pencils to decorate (optional)

INSTRUCTIONS

1. If you're using printed origami paper, put the plain side facing up. Fold it in half, corner-to-corner, then unfold it.
2. Fold the opposite two corners together.
3. Fold in along the dotted line.

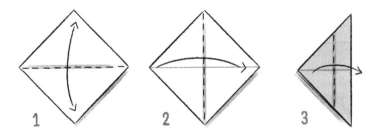

4. Fold out along the dotted line.

5. Pull one corner open to make a little square, then fold in half along the dotted line.

6. Fold one side, then the other, up along the dotted line. These are the wings.

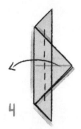 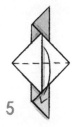

7. Fold the head down to make a crease, then fold it back again.

8. Press the point in, toward the chest of the bird, and crimp to make a beak. This is also called a "pocket fold."

9. Draw eyes and any other details you want on your dove. You might even want to write a message for peace!

9

Turn the page for a sneak peek of . . .

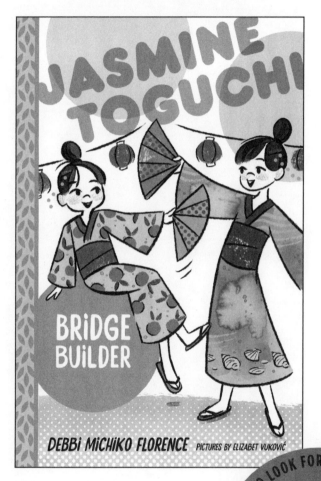

JASMINE TOGUCHI

BRIDGE BUILDER

DEBBI MICHIKO FLORENCE   PICTURES BY ELIZABET VUKOVIĆ

BE SURE TO LOOK FOR

JASMINE TOGUCHI
BRIDGE
BUILDER
COMING SOON!

PARADISE

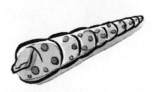

I stared out the window of the bus. We drove over a big bridge. I loved bridges. They connected one place to another. They were high up so you could see far-off things.

I looked down. Below us was the ocean. My big sister, Sophie, did not like being up high. It made her nervous. Next to me, she kept her eyes closed and listened to music on Mom's phone. Sophie said it was a good distraction.

We were spending most of our summer

vacation in Japan traveling. We took a plane from our home in Los Angeles to Tokyo. From Tokyo we took a super-fast train to Hiroshima to visit our grandma. Usually Obaachan comes to our house for New Year's and stays a whole month. This was our first time visiting her in Japan. We've been on subways and taxis and even a ferryboat. And we've done a *lot* of walking. Now we were on a bus.

I, Jasmine Toguchi, was on my way to a village called Kabo on an island called Suo Oshima. Obaachan grew up here before she moved to the United States. When Obaachan moved back to Japan though, she moved to Hiroshima. Her sister still lived in Kabo. Mom used to spend her summer vacations here. It was strange to think of Obaachan and Mom ever being my age.

"How much longer until we get there?" I asked Obaachan, who was sitting in front of us.

"We are almost there, Misa-chan," she said, calling me by my Japanese middle name.

I did not really believe her because Dad always said the same thing whenever we were driving some- where. "Almost there" always felt like forever.

I looked out the window again. After we crossed the bridge onto the island, the bus drove on a road right next to the ocean. The sun bounced off the sea, making little diamonds on the water. It was very pretty. It was almost like watching a movie.

The bus slowed down and came to a stop. I followed Mom and Dad, Sophie and Obaachan off the bus. After the bus driver unloaded our luggage, he drove away, leaving us in a small shelter.

"Where are we?" Sophie asked.

Across the road was a low wall.

"Go ahead," Dad said. "Take a peek."

Even though the road looked like a highway, there were no cars. Sophie took my hand. We looked both ways, then scurried across.

"Wowee zowee!" I said, leaning on the wall.

Below us were giant concrete blocks, a small sandy beach, and a big blue ocean. It was strange to see a beach with no people on it. At home in Los Angeles, when we went to the beach, it was always crowded. People sat on towels and beach chairs and blankets. Kids

played catch with balls or Frisbees. Families flew kites, built sandcastles, and waded in the ocean. Surfers rode the waves. It was busy and loud.

Here it was empty and quiet. Peaceful.

Mom came over and put her arms around our shoulders. "Beautiful, isn't it?" she said. "I came here almost every summer when I was your age. We always had the whole beach to ourselves."

It was like a paradise. Our very own paradise!

"Can we play on the beach?" I asked.

"Yes, but later," Mom said. "Let's go to the house. Your great-aunt, Yasuko Obaachan, is waiting. I haven't seen her in over ten years."

We crossed back to the bus stop. Dad and Obaachan were already walking away on a path, dragging their suitcases.

"We have to walk?" I asked. We walked a lot in Japan!

"It's not far," Mom promised.

Sophie and I grabbed our suitcases and followed Mom. We walked past a school. It had a huge yard.

"They have seesaws!" I shouted.

I have been wanting to ride a seesaw ever since I saw one at a park in Hiroshima. It looked like a long plank of wood with handles on both sides. You and a friend sat on opposite sides and went up and down.

"Sophie," I said, "will you ride with me?"

Sophie scrunched her nose. She did not like to be up high. I looked for Dad, but he and Obaachan were already far ahead of us.

I walked with Mom and Sophie, wishing Dad had waited for us.

"What is that?" I asked, looking down next to the path. Pointing is rude in Japan. I did not point, but  mostly because one hand was dragging my suitcase and the other hand was holding Fred Just Fred. Fred Just Fred was my second-favorite flamingo. I had to leave Felicia Flamingo at home because she is just as tall as me and would have been hard to carry around.

"These are rice paddies," Mom said. "This is how rice is grown."

I squinted at the field. The area was

flooded with water, and narrow green plants sprouted up.

"It doesn't look like rice," I said.

Sophie screeched next to my ear. I jumped in surprise. Mom grabbed my backpack so I didn't tumble into the rice paddy.

I turned to glare at my sister. "You almost made me fall!"

But Sophie didn't hear me. She was already running away. She flailed her arms around her head, screaming, "A giant bug!"

NOISY NATURE

I ran after Sophie. She had already caught up to Dad and Obaachan. I did not want her to get to the house before me.

"Matte!" I called out to her, telling her in Japanese to *wait*. I did not speak Japanese, but I knew some words. Sophie studied before we came to Japan, so she understood Japanese better than me. I was learning new words every day though.

It was very hot and sticky in Japan. I was

hot and sticky, too, by the time I caught up to Sophie at the top of the steep path. There was another narrow pathway that led to a house. Obaachan was talking to someone who looked almost like her. She wore a tan dress with a blue apron over it. She had short gray hair like puffy clouds. Black wire glasses perched on her nose, and her smile was wide, making her whole face light up like the sun.

Obaachan waved us over. "Hina-chan, Misa-chan, this is my sister and your great-aunt, Yasuko Obaachan."

Sophie and I bowed.

Mom and Dad finally caught up. They all laughed and talked very fast in Japanese. Their words skittered and skipped as their voices blended together.

"Doesn't Yasuko Obaachan speak English?" I asked quietly.

Dad patted my shoulder. "She's lived in Japan for so long without visiting the States

that she has forgotten most of her English. Obaachan talks with you both a lot. And she stays with us, so she gets to practice more often."

I took a deep breath. "It smells like oranges," I said.

Mom nodded to the area below us. "It's a tangerine grove. This island is known for their mikan."

"Wowee zowee!" I said. There were so many trees! "Can I climb one?"

Back home, Mrs. Reese, our neighbor, lets

me climb her apricot tree whenever I want. I use it as my thinking tree. I missed climbing and thinking.

"It's better that you don't," Mom said. "These trees are precious. Yasuko Obaachan grows and sells mikan. It's her job."

Sophie nudged me. "That means don't touch the trees, Squirt."

Squirt was the special name Sophie had for me when we were younger, when we were friends. All through her fifth-grade and my third-grade year, she was bossy and mean and ignored me a lot. But since we got to Japan, Sophie has been nicer. She started calling me Squirt again. Sophie and I were getting along and it made me happy! We were going to have so much fun together in Kabo!

We followed Yasuko Obaachan into the house. There was a dirt floor with a raised wood platform just like at Obaachan's house in Hiroshima. I knew what to do. I took off my shoes and climbed up into the house. The adults put on slippers, but Sophie and I stayed in our bare feet. The whole house had tatami floors. They looked like woven straw mats.

Yasuko Obaachan gave us a tour of the house. It had three main rooms: the eating area with a low table, a mostly empty room where we would all sleep, and another room where Yasuko Obaachan slept. Just like at Obaachan's house, all the doors slid open and shut. They reminded me of the doors that slid open to the backyard at my best friend Linnie Green's house. Except her doors were made of glass and you could see through them. The shoji doors here were made of wood and paper, and you could not see through them.

Thinking of Linnie made me miss her. We had never been apart this long. Good thing she gave me a journal before I left. I wrote in it like I was talking to her.

The house also had a kitchen, a bathroom,

and a bathing area. It had a Japanese bathtub just like at Obaachan's house. You take a bath outside the tub, splashing water on yourself.

We all sat down on zabuton, or cushions, at the low table. We snacked on crunchy cookies and drank hot tea.

At first Mom or Dad would tell me and Sophie what everyone was saying, since they were talking in Japanese. But after a while, Mom and Dad forgot to translate. I had no idea what was going on. I got bored as soon as the food was gone.

Sophie and I walked to the front room. The shoji doors to the house were all pushed open. It was like the house had no walls. We could see all the way down to the ocean, where we had gotten off the bus.

Even though we were in a village on a small island and even though there was no traffic or crowds of people, it was very, very loud.

"What is that noise?" I asked.

"Dad said insects." Sophie wrapped her arms around herself and shivered even though it was hot.

"Whoa," I said. "Those insects must be huge to make such loud sounds. Let's go explore!"

"Um." Sophie looked around the room. "I have to go to the bathroom!" she said as she rushed away.

I sat down to wait. My legs dangled over the edge of the house. I was not surprised Mom was so happy, chattering away with the family, but I also wished she noticed that I was sitting here alone.

Suddenly I heard Sophie scream.

Have you joined Jasmine on all of her adventures?
Check out these other stories featuring your favorite peace-maker!